THE STEWARD

A Parable For Those Who Tend the Future

For the next traveler.

First Edition
Printed in the United States of America
ISBN: 979-8-9989775-0-3

Published by
How to Be Alive Press
www.howtobealive.org

This is not a book.
This is a seed.

The Steward has no name,
for they are already within you.

May you walk the path,
plant what may outlast you,
and leave every place
better than you found it.

The journey does not end here.
It never does.

TABLE OF CONTENTS

THE VILLAGE THAT
CHASED SHADOWS

There was once a village where no one slept.

By day, they toiled endlessly. By night, they lay awake counting the things they had gathered. Stones. Shells. Bits of metal shaped like suns and moons.

They called these things wealth.

The villagers raced to pile their treasures higher than their neighbors. They locked their doors tightly.

They whispered of others stealing what was "rightfully theirs."

Yet still, none of them ever felt full.

The more they gathered, the more they feared losing.
The more they owned, the less they seemed to have.
It was as if they were chasing shadows under a moonless sky.

The village itself was plain.
No name carved above its gates.
No banners flown.
It could have been anywhere.
Or everywhere.

In this village lived a quiet one. No title. No wealth. No craving to compete.

They were called nothing special by others, but deep within, they held a restless question:

"What *is* wealth?"

A question no one else seemed to ask.
A question that refused to be silenced.

At night, they would sit just beyond the edge of the fields, watching the wind shape the tall grass into endless waves.

And they wondered.

Not yet knowing they were already standing at the beginning of a path.

THE QUESTION THAT
WOULD NOT LEAVE

The question traveled with them.

It moved like a silent companion, never far from their side.

In the market square, it tugged at their sleeve as others shouted of bargains and deals.

At the festival fires, it hovered like smoke in the night air while neighbors compared piles of tokens and treasures.

"What is wealth?"

No one seemed to notice the absurd dance around them.

The endless measuring. The silent competitions behind polite greetings.

The glances toward the heaviest coin pouch. The hunger behind the smiles.

The Steward
(for so we shall call them now)
tried once to ask aloud.

First to a merchant, whose cart bulged with silks and spices.

"What is wealth?" they said simply.

The merchant laughed without stopping his counting.

"Wealth is owning more than others,"
he replied, never looking up.
"It is the art of not being last."

The Steward walked on.

They asked an old farmer next, whose fields stretched farther than the eye could see.

"Wealth is land," the farmer grunted.
"The more you control, the safer you are."

Last, they asked a young child sitting by the fountain, playing with pebbles.
The child shrugged and smiled.

"Wealth?" the child echoed.
"I don't know. These pebbles are nice."

The Steward sat quietly beside the child for a long time.
The sun dipped low.
The stars whispered awake.

And the question only grew louder within them.

"If no one agrees, what truth have they really found?"

The next morning, before the village could stir, the Steward walked beyond the last stone boundary.

No map.
No companions.
No destination.

Only the question.

And the first step toward finding an answer.

THE QUIET DECISION

The village gates creaked as they swung open. The Steward stepped through without fanfare, without witness.

They carried no coin pouch. No map.

Only a small cloth bundle holding bread, a waterskin, and a smooth stone found at the edge of the field—their only keepsake.

Behind them, the village shrank with every footstep.
The sounds of bargaining and bartering faded into the morning mist.

Ahead lay only the vast unknown.

The first path led through fields of tall grasses that whispered to one another in the breeze.

The Steward listened.
They had learned that sometimes answers came not from people, but from the spaces in between.

At midday, they reached a fork where no signs stood.

One road wound toward distant smoke columns—another settlement perhaps.

The other disappeared into dense, ancient woods where sunlight barely kissed the forest floor.

The Steward sat.
They had always been taught:

"Go where others go. Stay where safety lies."

But the question inside would not allow it.

*"If wealth hides where everyone looks...
perhaps it lives where no one dares to seek."*

They stood.
Turned toward the woods.
And stepped into the shadows beneath the towering trees.

Without knowing, they had crossed a threshold.
The Journey had begun.

THE HOARDERS OF THE STONE VILLAGE

The forest thinned. The path widened.
At last, the Steward emerged at the edge of
a strange settlement.

The air itself felt heavy here.

Piles of smooth gray stones were stacked
along the pathways, in doorways, atop
roofs.

Some towers of stone reached toward the sky, swaying dangerously in the wind.

At the center of the village stood a great hall, its walls built from stones larger than any human could carry alone.

Around it, villagers scurried like ants, dragging more stones, polishing them, guarding them with wary eyes.

The Steward approached a bent old man struggling beneath the weight of three heavy rocks tied to his back.

"Why do you carry these?" the Steward asked gently.

The man looked up, startled, as if caught in some forbidden act of weakness.

"Stones are wealth," he whispered, glancing nervously over his shoulder.

"The more you possess, the greater your standing. Stones protect us. Stones define us."

As the Steward walked deeper into the village, the pattern repeated.
Children dragged pebbles in tiny carts.
Merchants sold stones polished to impossible smoothness.
Guards patrolled, watching for thieves who might steal even the smallest fragment.

And yet... the people moved with stooped shoulders.
Their faces wore deep lines of exhaustion.
They slept beside towering heaps yet shivered with fear of losing even one.

The Steward sat at the edge of the square and simply watched.
Hours passed. The pattern never changed.

A cold understanding settled in their chest:

"To build walls so high that no one may breach them... is also to build a prison without knowing."

As the sun slipped behind the distant trees, the Steward stood quietly.
They left the stone village as unnoticed as they had arrived.

The question remained.
But now it carried a new whisper:

"This is not the answer."

And so they walked on, toward the unknown.

THE DEBT CULT

The road narrowed again, winding through
barren fields.
Nothing grew here.
The soil lay cracked, thirsty under a
relentless sky.

At last the Steward came to a village
surrounded by towering wooden fences,
each plank carved with strange marks.

Inside, the houses leaned precariously, patched together with ropes and borrowed pieces of wood.

The villagers moved hurriedly, heads down, clutching thin slips of parchment.
They muttered numbers under their breath, their faces tense and hollow.

The Steward approached a woman who sat hunched by a broken well, staring at a scrap of paper with trembling hands.

"What is this place?" the Steward asked softly.

The woman didn't look up.

"The Village of Owed," she whispered.
"We live by the ledgers. We trade in promises and obligations. There is no wealth here, only debt."

The Steward frowned.

"What do you mean?"

The woman's voice cracked.

"I owe for my house. I owe for my food. I owe for my clothes. I owe for the air I breathe. My children will inherit my debts when I am gone."

The Steward wandered deeper into the village. At every corner stood "Collectors," dressed in dark robes, recording figures onto scrolls longer than the streets themselves.

No laughter filled the air.
No music.

Only the scratching of quills and the weary footsteps of those chasing balances they could never repay.

At sunset, the Steward sat quietly under a weathered tree at the village edge.
They watched as villagers exchanged slips of paper for food they could barely afford, always fearing the knock of the Collector.

A single thought echoed through the Steward's heart:

"To build an entire life around what is owed... is to never taste what is already yours."

With dawn came the choice.
The Steward stepped silently back onto the path, leaving the Village of Owed behind.

The question remained.
But the answer was not here.

THE GOLD CITY MIRAGE

The land flattened as the forest fell away.
Far ahead, the horizon glowed faintly even
under the midday sun.

The Steward walked toward the light.
As they crested the last hill, they saw it:

A city built entirely of shining gold.

Walls of gold bricks. Roofs of gold tiles. Even the cobblestones gleamed underfoot. Everywhere, gold reflected gold reflected gold.

The gates swung open easily, as if eager to swallow all who approached.

Inside, people bustled through crowded streets, arms heavy with ornaments, necklaces, coins, crowns. They smiled wide, laughed loud, gestured broadly.

But their eyes flicked constantly to the passersby, measuring, comparing, calculating.

The Steward paused to watch.

Two men argued over who wore the heavier chain.

A woman wept because another's robe shimmered more brightly.
Children fought over who would inherit the largest ring.

Everywhere, the same silent hunger remained beneath the gilded surface.
The fear of falling behind.
The terror of being outshined.

The Steward approached a jeweler polishing a mountain of golden trinkets.

"Why do you gather so much?"

The jeweler didn't look up.

"Because others gather more."

The Steward wandered deeper into the city, searching for something real.

A tree. A bird. A river.
Nothing lived here but gold.

Even the air felt stale, heavy, as if exhausted by constant display.

At sunset, the city blazed brilliantly against the darkening sky, a final desperate show before nightfall.

The Steward stood at the edge and whispered the truth only the wind could hear:

"To build a city of gold is to forget the warmth of soil, the song of water, the breath of life. It dazzles, but does not nourish."

Without looking back, they slipped quietly into the shadows.

The city of gold glimmered behind them,
still shining, still hollow.

The question remained.
But the answer was not here.

THE SCARCITY MONKS

The forest closed in again.
The golden shimmer of the city vanished
behind thick trunks and twisting roots.

The Steward walked for many days in
silence.
Then, faintly through the mist, came the
soft echo of bells.

They followed the sound to a clearing where simple stone huts formed a perfect circle.
No walls. No gates. No possessions visible anywhere.

At the center stood a weathered figure in gray robes, head bowed, sweeping the dirt with a bundle of dried reeds.

The Steward approached.

"What is this place?"

The figure looked up slowly, eyes calm but distant.

"This is the Order of Less," the monk said softly.
"We own nothing. We desire nothing. In emptiness, we find purity."

The Steward stayed for several days.

They watched as the monks refused gifts,
slept on bare ground, drank only rainwater,
ate only wild herbs.

The villagers nearby whispered of their
wisdom.
Yet the Steward noticed something beneath
the still surface.

Hunger in the hollow cheeks.
Tension behind soft smiles.

Quiet judgments cast toward anyone
carrying even the smallest token from the
outside world.

The Steward sat one night with an elder
monk beneath the moonlit sky.

"Why do you reject everything?" they asked.

The elder's gaze hardened.

> *"To possess is to fall into corruption. All things lead to attachment. Better to own nothing, to need nothing."*

The Steward looked at the trees swaying gently, exchanging breath with the stars.
The forest did not hoard, nor did it deny itself completely.

It gave. It received. It cycled freely.

The Steward bowed with gratitude, then rose before dawn.
As they stepped beyond the clearing, the wind whispered the lesson:

To deny all is merely the mirror of grasping all.
Both are prisons built of fear.

The path ahead vanished into fog.
The Steward followed, knowing the answer
still lay beyond.

THE CHILD BY THE RIVER

The path wandered downward into a quiet valley.
There, a slow, clear river wound its way through fields of tall grass and wildflowers.

The Steward followed its gentle curves, listening to the water speak in soft rhythms older than memory.

As the sun drifted low, they came upon a child sitting at the river's edge.
The child was stacking small stones, letting them tumble back into the water with a laugh each time the tower collapsed.

The Steward smiled and sat nearby.
For a long time, neither spoke.

At last, the Steward broke the silence.

"Why do you let the stones fall?"

The child looked up, grinning.

*"Because they always do.
And then I get to build again."*

The Steward watched the next tower fall.
The laughter that followed was light, unburdened, free.

"What is wealth to you?" the Steward asked
softly.

The child paused, tilted their head
thoughtfully, then shrugged.

> *"Maybe... the fun of stacking.*
> *And the fun of letting go."*

The wind rippled across the river.
The Steward closed their eyes.
The simplicity held more truth than all the
ledgers, gold towers, and empty
renunciations combined.

When the Steward opened their eyes again,
the child was gone.
Only a single smooth stone remained at the
water's edge.

The Steward picked it up.

On its surface, faint lines seemed to shimmer in patterns only partly understood.

They turned it over reverently.

A single line of words was carved into the stone:

You cannot possess the river.
You cannot stop its flow.
You can only stand in wonder, and drink.

The Steward placed the stone gently back where it belonged.
Then rose, and followed the river onward.

The question remained.

But for the first time, the Steward smiled.

THE RAVEN AND THE FIELD

The river eventually vanished into the folds of the land, leaving the Steward standing at the edge of a vast, open field.

Golden grasses swayed like an ocean beneath the endless sky.
There were no walls here. No markets. No voices.

Only wind. And the faint caw of a raven far above.

The Steward walked slowly through the tall grass, breathing the wide, wild silence.
For the first time in their journey, there was nothing to compare, nothing to measure.

A shadow passed overhead.
The raven circled once, twice, then landed on a weathered fence post ahead.

Its black feathers shimmered violet in the sun.
Its eyes held something ancient and unblinking.

The Steward approached cautiously.

The raven spoke—not with words, but with knowing.

"You seek the answer to wealth."

The Steward nodded.

The raven tilted its head.

"You've seen the hoarders, the debt keepers,
the gold seekers, the deniers.
All built rigid systems around fear."

The Steward's brow furrowed.

"If those are not wealth... then what is?"

The raven flapped its wings once, then settled.

"Watch."

The bird lifted off, soaring high.

Below, the wind rippled through the grasses.
The Steward stared.

The field bent and flowed, dancing effortlessly.
No blade resisted.
No stalk tried to stand above the rest.
Together, they rose and fell in perfect harmony.

The Steward stood motionless.
The lesson was unmistakable:

Wealth is not static.
Wealth moves.
It flows, shifts, breathes.
It is never meant to be trapped or frozen.

The raven circled once more, then vanished into the vast sky.

At the Steward's feet lay a small feather.

They picked it up.

Etched faintly along the shaft were words barely visible in the fading light.

Life flows.
Wealth flows.
The attempt to stop either
is the beginning of loss.

The Steward turned toward the horizon.
The grasses parted gently with each step as they walked on.

The question remained.
But the answer was drawing closer.

THE GARDENER'S LESSON

The field gave way to a small garden tucked between two rolling hills.
It was unlike anything the Steward had yet encountered.

Neat rows of vegetables and herbs grew beside wild patches of flowers and towering sunflowers.

Vines wove freely between trees heavy with fruit.
Butterflies and bees drifted lazily from bloom to bloom.

At the center knelt an elderly gardener, sleeves rolled up, hands deep in the dark, living soil.

The Steward approached quietly and watched as the gardener worked—not dominating, not controlling, but guiding the growth with gentle intention.

The gardener glanced up, eyes warm and crinkled at the corners.

"You've come a long way to find something you already carry."

The Steward smiled faintly.

"I've seen what wealth is not.
But I still do not know what it is."

The gardener wiped their hands and gestured broadly to the living canvas before them.

"Wealth is not what you take.
Wealth is what you tend."

The Steward knelt beside them and together they worked in silence.
Weeding here. Loosening soil there.
Watering gently.
Each act small.
Each act meaningful.

"The seed holds no promise unless placed into the ground," the gardener said softly.

"The tree bears no fruit unless cared for over seasons, even if you will not live to taste it."

The gardener reached into their pocket and pressed something into the Steward's palm. A tiny seed.

"The only true wealth," they whispered, *"is that which multiplies by being given away."*

Carved faintly into the shell of the seed were ancient words.

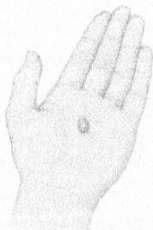

You cannot keep a seed.
You can only plant it.
That is the beginning of wealth.

The Steward held the seed tightly for a long moment.
Then bowed deeply to the gardener.

With the first stars blinking into existence above, they stepped once more onto the winding path.

The question remained.
But its shape was changing.

THE NIGHT UNDER THE GREAT TREE

The path grew steep and narrow.
The air cooled as twilight deepened into night.

At the crest of a gentle hill stood a single towering tree.
Its ancient branches twisted skyward like open hands reaching for something long forgotten.

The roots plunged deep into the earth as if anchoring the heavens to the soil.

The Steward approached slowly.
Exhausted.
The weight of all they had seen pressing inward like heavy stone.

They sat at the base of the tree and stared into the emptiness of the dark horizon.
No hoarders.
No debt keepers.
No gold chasers.
No monks of denial.

Only silence.
Only stars.
Only the rhythmic whisper of leaves shifting high above.

The Steward bowed their head into their hands and exhaled.

"I have walked far and learned much.
Yet I am no closer to an answer than when I
began."

The wind stirred.
The leaves shivered like distant bells.
No reply came.

The Steward closed their eyes.
For the first time, they surrendered completely.
Not to failure.
Not to despair.
But to unknowing.

They drifted into sleep as the stars spun slowly overhead.

And in the space where dreams and waking meet, something shifted.
No voice spoke.
No figure appeared.

Yet the understanding poured in like water
filling an empty vessel:

Wealth was never meant to be possessed.
It was never meant to be measured.
It was never meant to be hoarded,
chased, or denied.

Wealth is life-force itself.
Energy that moves through all things.
A current, a seed, a breath.
It multiplies only when given.
It exists only in motion.
It lives only in release.

At dawn, the Steward awoke beneath soft
golden light filtering through the branches.
In their hand rested a single smooth stone,
cool and solid yet impossibly light.
Etched into its surface were the final words.

The Wealth That Cannot Be Kept

You can build walls or you can plant seeds.
You can cling or you can give.
Wealth flows.
Life flows.
Be the river.

The Steward stood slowly, filled with quiet clarity. They placed the stone gently at the base of the tree.

Then, lighter than they had ever felt, they turned toward the path that led home.

The question remained.
But this time, so did the answer.

THE RETURN WITHOUT WORDS

The path home was the same, yet not the same.

The fields still waved softly under the morning breeze.
The river still carved its patient course through the valley.
The distant shapes of the village rooftops appeared over the hills as they always had.

Yet everything felt different.
Lighter.
Clearer.
Alive.

The Steward walked quietly through the village gates.
No heralds announced their arrival.
No crowd awaited.

The marketplace bustled just as before.
Merchants bartered.
Neighbors gossiped.
Coins changed hands.

The Steward smiled gently.
They had no desire to interrupt the dance.

Instead, they began in the smallest of ways.
They shared seeds with those who had none.
They taught children how to tend the soil.

They repaired the broken well so water could flow freely again.

They gave without fanfare, modeled without preaching.

Some villagers watched with confusion.

Others imitated, though they did not yet understand why.

Over time, small shifts began.

The heavy stones that had once lined doorways were quietly dismantled.

The ledgers of debts gathered dust, replaced by shared harvests.

Even the gold charms faded beneath the colors of blooming gardens.

The Steward never claimed credit.

They asked for nothing.

They simply moved, acted, tended.

In every gesture, they had become what the raven and the gardener had shown:

Be the river.
Be the seed planter.
Be the one who gives so that others may one day give too.

As the sun slipped behind the hills, the Steward walked alone to the far edge of the village.
They stood for a long moment beneath the stars, breathing deeply of the cool night air.

There was no need to stay.
The work had only just begun... elsewhere.

With calm certainty, the Steward stepped once more onto the open path.

The journey continued.

THE AWAKENING OF THE VILLAGE

Seasons passed.

The villagers never could agree on when exactly the change had begun.
There had been no grand speech, no decree from the elders, no monument erected.

But slowly, unmistakably, something shifted.

The fields grew greener.
The once-barren plots now teemed with vegetables, herbs, and flowers.
Neighbors shared tools and seeds without keeping tally.
Children laughed as they helped plant saplings along the riverbank.

The heavy stone towers once hoarded at doorways had quietly vanished.
No one spoke of where they had gone.
No one missed them.

The marketplace still bustled, yet the energy had softened.
Fewer shouted.
More smiled.
People traded not only goods, but time, skills, care.

A merchant offered baskets of grain to those who had none.

A farmer taught an apprentice how to mend soil.

An elder wove blankets for newborns without asking payment.

The Steward had long since disappeared down some distant path.

But their presence lingered like the warmth of a fire after the flames had gone.

Villagers began to speak of *The Way of the Steward*—not as a rigid teaching, but as a quiet understanding:

Give when you can.
Plant what may outlast you.
Leave every place better than you found it.

The Steward had become not a person, but an archetype.

A possibility within anyone.

One evening, as the last light faded over the horizon, a young traveler arrived at the village gates.

Worn sandals.
Empty hands.
A question burning quietly behind soft eyes.

The villagers smiled.
They knew.

The cycle had begun again.

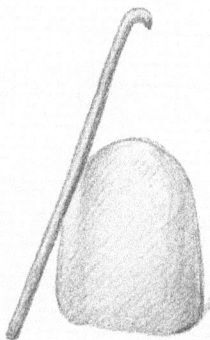

THE NEXT TRAVELER

The road stretched beyond the village,
winding into misty hills and distant valleys
unseen.

At the edge of the worn path stood a lone
figure.
Young or old, it was hard to say.
Not male or female, but simply *becoming*.

Their clothes were plain.
Their pack nearly empty.
Only a small seed rested in their palm.

The villagers had offered food, maps, and advice.
The traveler had smiled politely, thanked them, and declined.

They gazed at the horizon.
Then at the seed.
Then back again.

No crowd gathered.
No ceremony marked the moment.

Only a question, unspoken but alive:

"What is wealth?"

The wind answered by stirring the tall grasses into waves.

The river far below whispered its ancient truth.

The great tree stood somewhere out there, waiting.

The traveler smiled.
Took a single step forward.

And disappeared into the Drift.

The journey does not end here.
It never does.

The Steward walks onward.
Now, so do you.